HAN M GREENBARG

Firemartenn

League Of Martenns: Book One

First published by starlighteineadhpress 2022

This novel is entirely a work of fiction. The names, characters and incidents portrayed in it are the work of the author's imagination. Any resemblance to actual persons, living or dead, events or localities is entirely coincidental.

First edition

ISBN: 979-8-98-660442-8

This book was professionally typeset on Reedsy.
Find out more at reedsy.com

Contents

1

Honor Ceremony

I'm supposed to be the most special one in Ateinekus. But no one looks at me. Not the elders, not my teachers, not Mother. Father can't look at me because he is dead. My schoolmates just beat me up. I'm not respected. Not loved. Or is it because they are afraid? I am part dragon after all. A Martenn. It's rare to be born a Martenn, but I am one.

I just turned eight today, and I'm late for the Honor ceremony. Father arrived late to his ceremony so I think it's only fair that I get to do the same. The elders won't mind. They never mind. I already know what my power is. It's fire. I just have to prove it to them. Especially to Fintspeik. He dislikes me most.

"We have been standing here for three hours, boy." Edaiewkk sounds grumpier than usual. "What in the name of Otrusc have you been doing?"

I slow down in my approach. Fintspeik and Augiett are holding behemoth torches on either side of the ehreleit, clearly irritated at my tardiness. "This is absolute blakinsok, Jhetsam!"

I laugh at them using the Martenn word for *nonsense*. "I thought you hated the Martenn language, Masters."

"We do, but if it's the only thing that will get through your ears, little firebreath, I will utter dreadful Martenn words."

"I was catching rats for my dinner. Mother won't catch them for me. She says they're horrid."

"This ceremony should matter more to you than eating rat."

"Already ate one on the way over," I say proudly. It was a very agile catch too.

"Ugh." Edaiewkk scowls. He has the same disgusted look on his face as Mother does when she listens to me devour my food. None of the villagers eat rats. Only goblins share my love of them. I have way more in common with goblins than I do with Elves.

I shrug the frayed black cloak off my shoulders and step onto the middle of the ehreleit, facing Otrusc's Dome. Violet flame torches crackle along the twin stone paths that curve into a circle before the large stone platform. A patch of red petal flowers sprinkled with an endless ash rain lays to the right of it.

"Jet Jhetsam, son of Junilier and Keissagsa, has chosen to dedicate himself to the quest of retrieving Ackellhnn's sapphire. Just as his father sacrificed, so will he forfeit the life of a civilian." Fintspeik makes deranged circles with veiny hands in the air as he speaks to the gathered elders, his bellowing coughs punctuating each word. The old pipe smoker's cough.

"Do you take this honor of your own will?"

Risking groans of disapproval, I answer in a small but loud voice, "I'm going to finish my father Junilier's road. I vow it."

The elders trade wry smiles.

"And," I say, "I will not die like he did."

"How can you be certain?" Fintspeik asks.

"Otrusc. His body is buried under this bed of rock. I feel power from it."

"Reckless magician, are we?"

"No magic. Strength." I do as I've seen the elders do, tapping my fist twice against my chest. "In here."

"The strength of one's heart is not enough to walk into Aeissfaud. You must mature, boy."

"Eamt sarftiiak." *I'm strong.*

"Common speak, Jhetsam," Fintspeik snaps at me. "No Martenn words here."

"Eamt sarftiiak," I say again. "You spoke a Martenn word a few minutes ago, Master."

"One," he growls. "I spoke one word, Jhetsam!"

Blakinsok. I smile to myself. He said my favorite Martenn word.

"Prove to us that you are a Firemartenn. Set yourself alight," Edaiewkk says in his hollow, breathy voice.

I see Fintspeik pass his torch to another elder so he can steal a bottle of blackberry wine from Edaiewkk. He sips it and his annoyingly sharp cough sounds out again.

"Okay," I whisper. "I can do this. I'm doing this. Feurix-maratgnn. Feurixmaratgnn." *Firemartenn. Firemartenn.* "I am a Firemartenn." Several strands of hair fall into my eyes as I lift my head. I cross my arms, laying my palms flat against my shoulders.

I breathe out hard, sending a thin swirl of smoke and flame onto the branches laid around my feet. I snort out flame, feeling a warm tingle in my nostrils. My arms drop to my sides and my hands clench into fists. The fire is crawling up, engulfing me. The fire that I made. Proof enough. The elders should be proud.

"Jet," Edaiewkk calls out amidst a funny sounding belch, "you have the gift. You have the confidence. But you have much more to learn about the Martenns. Far more than any one of us can teach you."

I shake my head. "I know enough, Master."

"In time, yes, I believe you will." Edaiewkk picks up the pail of water near the ehreleit and tosses it in the air. I'm drenched. "We will bring you to your mentor when you're of age."

"What mentor?" I ask between chattering teeth.

Fintspeik briefly looks at Edaiewkk before answering. "Desorfk."

"Who's that?"

"The one who trained your father."

I step off the ehreleit, the taste of flame and ash coating my throat and tongue. I wonder when I'll get to meet Desorfk and wonder why I have to wait so long to go to Aeissfaud. The elders are walking away from Otrusc's Dome. No one congratulates me on showing off my power. The ceremony is done. A bit disappointing really. And I have to go home to Mother who is just one more person that doesn't care.

"Hey, dragonbrain!"

I look over my shoulder to see who's calling me. Dymraus. The tyrannical leader of the Fire Whelps Brigade.

Oh no. All six of them are with him this time.

"Jet, that was amazing. How about you show me how to breathe fire like that?"

Running usually works, but Dymraus looks like he wants to try to drain my blood again. That determination in his face worries me.

"You're such a little thing, dragonbrain. No muscle. No wings."

I circle back as he comes forward. He's two years older than me and two feet taller.

"Elf-dragons don't have wings. We look just like you," I say.

"Show me your fire breath."

"No."

"C'mon. Show me how to do it."

"You can't. You're not an Elf-dragon."

"What if we were brothers bound by blood? You give me some of your dragon blood, Jet, and I won't ask you ever again."

I breathe out slow, a wisp of smoke exiting my mouth. Dymraus grins and brandishes a serrated knife.

"You can't have my blood," I whisper.

"Because we're lowlifes, right? Nobody's better than the Firemartenn. You get all the power. All the glory. Right?"

I turn to stare at the rest of them, then I run.

"Bring him to the ehreleit!" Dymraus yells to his horrible clan.

The safest place I know is a lava hare's burrow dug just beyond the northern village gate. I've used it as a hiding spot ever since I could crawl. But I don't make it half a league before they grab hold of me and violently drag me back to the ehreleit. I'm small for my age. I can't do anything other than scream for help. But I don't scream. They can't know I'm scared.

"Hold the Firemartenn down," Dymraus orders. "We get all his blood."

I never use my fire breath as a weapon. I don't want to hurt anyone. But Dymraus sounds more vicious this time. Deadly vicious. Like he wants to kill me.

"Do we get to use our knives too?"

"Shut up, Zheaurm. I'm doing this."

They have me literally bound to the ehreleit. All I can do is listen to their conversation above me. There's more than one knife. They're going to sacrifice me.

"Do it fast."

"What's the hurry? He's not even screaming."

"He will. Little dragonbrain's gonna wake up the whole village."

No one will come for me and I'm about to be bled out by a crazy bunch of power-hungry elflings. I'm breathing so fast, can't get proper air in my lungs. Dizzy. My arms and legs are convulsing.

"Get ready to be blood brothers, Jet," Dymraus says with a sneer.

My life can't be over already. I just had my Honor ceremony.

"Feurixmaratgnn," I whisper through chattering teeth. "Feurixmaratgnn."

A feeling I've never had jolts through my trembling body, and I breathe out a steady line of fire. A directionless angry wind surges around me. Hot, dry, wild. I can't control my fire. Inferno. I'm in an inferno.

"It's burning! Get out!"

"There's no water!"

"Fintspeik, the rock pile! Crush the rocks!"

"Where the dragmite is that little firebreath?"

The villagers are screaming. Every structure in Ateinekus is in flames. Dymraus and his clan have run away. But I don't see anything except for a massive dragon.

There's a dragon looking right at me.

An Aludenwolke.

2

Aludenwolke

Smoke and ash cover everything in Ateinekus. People are running around us in a panic calling out to their children. Ember-filled houses. Not even an eruption from the Aeissfaud volcanoes has touched the village like this. But all I see is the dragon. A she-dragon.

"Priteag, wundeircha," I whisper as I reach up to touch her. *Hello, beautiful.* The violet scales aren't rough like I thought they would be. They're soft. She nuzzles her head against my hand.

"Eamt Jet. Kakyeti lurr neidascha?" *I'm Jet. What's your name?*

"Fluri," she says, her voice soothing and melodic like a bumblebee's hum.

"Fluri," I repeat. "Wundeircha." *Beautiful.*

She dips her large head, tossing the silky red mane over her silver eyes. Aludenwolke aren't the largest or most powerful of dragon breeds, but they are the most visually stunning.

Angry voices suddenly sound out through the haze. The elders.

"Hoschir mitk mehii," Fluri says. *Fly with me.* She motions with her head for me to get on her back.

"Sameitle?" *Really?*

"Komm. Terve ottun mehii." *Come. Hold onto me.*

"Dachebriven ruhgel fanruttiln," I say. *Dragons stay underground.* I don't understand why she is risking her life. "Ahnj scha lue hayn?" *Why are you here?*

"Komm, einalkyv Feurixmaratgnn." *Come, little Firemartenn.* The elders are after me. No time for arguing.

"Avlai." *Okay.* I crouch on Fluri's back, gripping her mane as she ascends faster than any breathing creature can. We're flying further and further above Ateinekus. I almost fall off as she goes vertical, but I don't panic. The spark of a new energy thunders within my body.

"Delka lue maechev vate feurixgrozt?" I ask. *Did you make that firestorm?*

"Vate beel aky lue, Feurixmaratgnn. Aludenwolke daet aidyat feurix." *That was all you, Firemartenn. Aludenwolke don't breathe fire.*

"Eaemt doppvat roflued," I groan to myself. *I'm double cursed.* "Nae guthost." *Not good.*

"Suchopni uth." *Look up.* She's trying to distract me from the destruction below. "Suchopni traap tun fer votind." *Look there to the east.*

I finally draw in a breath of fresh air, noticing a faint line of mountains piercing the clouds. The other side of Ervenfuge. "Kakyet ivv vate?" *What is that?*

"Felssuzkit Bergekletten." *Felssuzkit Mountains.*

"Lurnh ulka edni?" *Can we go?*

"Wheyta lurrk altashn," she says. *When you're older.*

I think Fluri's sounding a bit too much like Mother, but I have a lot of questions. "Ahnj delka lue komm hayn?" *Why did you come here?*

"Ea edni wraichdt ea khoauch." *I go where I want.*

"Ben fernlaty imliatt lue." *But they'll kill you.*

"Lue wardhi lozzt esdauv, Feurixmaratgnn." *You won't let them, Firemartenn.*

"Rufite mehii Jet." *Call me Jet.*

"Gobeir tun hoschir svezkru, Jet?" she asks. *Ready to fly upside down, Jet?* Her voice is excited. I can tell that we're about to do something really fun.

"Eamt gobeir," I say. *I'm ready.*

"Terve ott!" *Hold on!*

I grip her mane tighter, leaning my face into her neck. She's breathing loudly as she dives down and sharply turns right, throwing us into an endless back flip. I can't figure out which way is up until I tilt my head back and see that my hair is grazing the ground. I'm upside down. We're upside down in the air.

"Lurrk einaunli," I call out. *You're amazing.*

"Eavek mipriuv lue zurchs heinay. Gehanha ikdisatz." *I'll bring you back home. Secret landing.*

Back home. I don't want to go back down there. They're all angry. But the she-dragon can't fly forever. "Fluri, ahnj delka lue komm tun mehii?" *Fluri, why did you come to me?*

"Lurrk fer Feurixmaratgnn. Ulka chufuel lurr silamacht." *You're the Firemartenn. We feel your power.*

"Ulka?" *We?*

"Aky dachebriven. Ulka scha aivi gobeir udt lurr lehfmodae." *All dragons. We are getting ready for your command.*

"Kakyet lehfmodae?" *What command?*

"Lue wil chahren riv." *You will learn it.*

My mind goes to Dymraus and his friends. "Delka fernlat hegti andi weilouv I lue?" *Did they run away because of you?*

"Ay," she says with a toss of her head. *Yes.*

"Fernlat waln ednibahn tun nehebr mlae kronvey. Lue sokregen mehii." *They were going to take my blood. You saved me.*

"Lue schulprivn mehii neichadu." *You owe me nothing.*

After I slide off her back, I turn to look up at her. She is one of the slender dragon breeds, her body more like that of a horse than a muscular, scaly beast, but she still towers over the smoldering village. I have to tilt my head all the way back to see her face.

"Wil lue ruhgel?" *Will you stay?*

She doesn't speak.

"Wundeircha," I whisper with a smile. "Mlae wundeircha." *My beautiful.*

Fluri swishes her tail, slamming it into the roof of my house and snorting right before taking off into the night. I keep my gaze up, searching for any stars, envious of the she-dragon being able to fly away. There is no light in the village. Only smoke. The smell of burning flesh and wood.

"Jhetsam!" the elders scream.

I'm powerless as they rush toward me. I know it's a lost battle.

"You're rebuilding everything, you hear me? Everything, you firebreath rat!"

The fun is over tonight.

3

Meeting Desorfk

<u>Seven Years Later</u>

"Eavek syatre lue sonnkhtja, wundeircha. Daet lozzt esdauv ki lue." *I'll meet you at sunrise, beautiful. Don't let them see you.*

"Ea neichty dai," she says. *I never do.*

With no breaks in flight, we should get to Anteonviik in two days. I'm so excited about leaving home with my she-dragon. She's the only one who has been there to defend me through years of bloodletting attacks I've endured by my classmates. They still believe that they'll get wings and fire breath just by torturing me. Me. The lithe Firemartenn. I hate being the victim.

"Ardavii udt mehii, Fluri." *Wait for me, Fluri.*

Fluri joyfully snorts and prances in place like a feisty mare, the force of her legs and talons in the dirt sending an earthquake toward the village center.

"Shh." I motion for her to lay low as I crawl back under the metal fence.

Hollow drums sound out in the dry air, the symphonic noise sending me sprinting back home. The elders know that a dragon is moving freely in Ateinekus, and they make certain to blame me for any damage that she causes. I usually like to pretend that I don't know what they're talking about because for all we know it could be a volcanic eruption that shook the ground. We're less than five leagues from Aeissfaud and our entire region is filled with lava and rock rain.

I grin as I walk by Edaiewkk, who scowls as he leans on a charred door frame, his pipe in hand.

"Time with the dragon girlfriend, you spider-haired filth," he says to me. "Disgusting."

I pick at a dead spider crumpled on my scalp, thinking to save it and drop it on someone's walkway. Spider-haired indeed. At least one volcanic insect always follows me home, and in the years before turning fifteen, I spent many a night planting the hairy little critters around the village to give the snobby people a scare.

I'm hated even more since the firestorm… everyone blames me for their losses. I try to do one nice thing a day for Mother, even if it means sitting with her and drinking the awful tea she makes. Tonight I choose to scrub dishes, talking to myself while Mother stares blankly at the kitchen table.

"Best son ever," I mumble as I place a clean tankard on a shelf. "Doing dishes without water. How do I do this? Oh, right, I use the power of rocks to disintegrate crumbs and berry stains. You're an expert now, Jet. Total expert. You should get payment for this."

Mother is silent. I can hear her sipping tea behind me.

"Did you have a good day, Jet?" I ask myself. "Oh, I had an adventure of a day. Running around with my she-dragon and being up to no good. I bet Mother would kick me out if I brought Fluri over." I grin thinking of how I must have rattled Mother by mentioning Fluri. Maybe if she took a ride in the clouds she would change her mind about dragons. After all, there's no better feeling than flying.

The brisk knocking of Fintspeik and Edaiewkk jolts me from

my thoughts. They have a habit of announcing themselves together when they're going to tell on me to Mother, so I have to assume I'm in trouble again.

"Keissagsa," Fintspeik calls out. He walks in first and stands in front of Mother. "Jet's mentor asks for him."

Edaiewkk stares down at the pile of dishes I have yet to scrub. "A little slow at that, aren't you, boy?"

My mentor… I'm going to meet my mentor.

"It's time," Fintspeik says. He lowers his voice when Mother looks up from her tea. "He must come with us."

Mother's eyes meet mine, and I'm startled when she speaks with a trembling voice. "Jet's just a child."

"Age isn't relevant, Keissagsa. You know this."

"Junilier was halfway to a thousand when he left."

"It is not our decision. His mentor decides when he's ready." With a quick wrist flick, Edaiewkk motions for me to follow them.

Mother stays at the table staring at me in a way she's never done before. I know that expression on anyone. She's scared.

"Desorfk waits for you, Jhetsam."

"Now?"

"Yes."

I don't know what to say to Mother. If I should say anything at all. I start to move around the house, packing anything I think would be useful for a long journey, but Fintspeik barks out, "you bring nothing. Come."

"Don't I get to carry a knife at least?"

"No."

I look again at Mother, seeing her sip her tea as if this was all a normal scene in her house. But I can tell that she's pretending. She's never cared to hug me or see me off to school so I know she won't pay attention to me walking out the door, but she still looks scared.

"Come, Firemartenn."

The two of them make certain I exit the house empty-handed and guide me through the village. Suddenly I feel more like a powerful dignitary than a problem child.

"Where are we going?"

"Just follow," Fintspeik says.

They stop in front of the local butcher shop and I'm more confused than ever. First of all, I don't ever go in there because I'm the hunter of my own food. Secondly, most Elves in Ateinekus choose chalky limestone tea and charred bread over meat.

"He's here," Edaiewkk states sharply. "Jhetsam, whatever you do, please refrain from making jokes. It's life or death."

"Sure, Master, but if one of you elders is taking me into Aeissfaud, I really hope you kept up your agility. You're all too old for this sort of thing."

Fintspeik shakes his head at my teasing grin. "Your mentor is not an Elf of Ateinekus, boy."

"What is he then?"

They gesture for me to go ahead of them through the doorway, clearly trying to hasten my departure from the village.

"Jet son of Junilier," Edaiewkk announces.

The butcher doesn't respond, aggressively slamming his knife into a mountain pheasant. He's not what I expected to see and clearly I'm not worthy of him stopping his work to greet me.

"Desorfk?" I ask.

He glances up, meeting my eyes as he holds the knife above his head. "Aye," he says, and continues hacking up the bird.

Desorfk looks like a typical goblin, but his voice is deeper, more raspy. Their sharp teeth and orange eyes make them look mean, but each one I've met has been soft-hearted. Judging by his crooked gray shoulders and stiff little legs, Desorfk looks like he's been through multiple wars.

"You two may leave," he says, giving a hard stare at the elders.

Neither Edaiewkk nor Fintspeik move from their place by the door. Desorfk glances at me again, sending a silent message that I interpret to mean he wants my help in kicking them out. Without hesitation, I grab some raw venison off the table and flamboyantly eat it, horrifying the both of them.

"Dragon blood indeed," Desorfk says as he watches them sprint outside. He gives a toothy grin and offers me a piece of raw pheasant.

"Are you really my mentor?" I ask. "Or are you just filling in for someone?"

He silently turns around, walking toward the fire at the back of the shop. I wonder if I just said something wrong. I don't think I did. "Do other Martenns have mentors?"

"Their mentors are the dragons."

I chew on a new piece of meat, confused when Desorfk returns to his knife work. "Why isn't mine a dragon?"

He motions for me to lean in and whispers, "It is, Jet. I'm just the messenger."

"Really?"

"Keep your voice low. I'm betting those two are still pacing around out there."

"I'm going to see the Feurix?"

"The Feurix king himself," Desorfk says. "Feuskarg."

"For real?"

"Yes."

"Do the elders know?"

He grins like we're in on a secret together. "They know I'm a tricky durarset."

"Well," I say, "I guess all goblins are a little bit foolish."

"So are Firemartenns."

I grin back. The thought of meeting Feuskarg is overwhelming my mind. I won't be able to think or speak of anything else for days or weeks.

"Ever try cinder wine?"

"No."

Desorfk pours steaming red liquid into a cup and slides it toward me. "Go on."

I'm stunned at being offered wine. Mother would thrash me if she knew I had tried some. But this is from my new goblin friend. Best day ever.

"Drink it, Jet." He has a mischievous gleam in his eyes as he watches me eagerly put it up to my mouth. "Ash and berries floating in magma."

I sputter and he laughs. "You get used to it."

"I just didn't expect it to sting so much."

Desorfk nods and points to a crack in the wall near the fire. "It's from the core of Irakkitide. The volcano's tunnel reaches here and I get the magma to drink. It's good for an energy kick."

"Wow," I say, coughing as he pours more into the cup. "That's intense."

"The real fun is when you get the other Martenns to drink it. They can't handle heat like you and I can." He looks straight up into my eyes. "Feurix blood. That's what you carry. It's the reason you caused that firestorm."

Oh no. Not this again. "You know about that?"

"I was in it. We all were."

"Were you hurt?"

"Nah," he says. "Goblins are flame-resistant."

"Everyone hates me for that night."

Desorfk listens while cutting up the venison, his large, fox-like ears tilting toward my voice.

"I'm ready to get away from the elders," I say. "Away from my problems here."

He looks seriously at my face. Doesn't say anything. I watch him cut meat for a while, unsure of how I'm supposed to reach the Feurix. Is he taking me there? Do I find them on my own? Why is he taking so long in cutting meat?

"How good is your Maratgnn?" he asks.

I don't answer right away. He should know that I speak like the dragons. He knows I'm a Firemartenn.

"Jet, how good is your Maratgnn?" he repeats.

"Eamt liifenka." *I'm fluent.*

"Mehii tunn." *Me too.*

"You know the Martenn language?"

"I lead Firemartenns to the fire dragons. Of course I know it." He drinks his own cup of cinder wine before changing his demeanor to that of a boring teacher. "Maratgnn is also known as what?"

"Dragonspeak."

"Yes. The dragons spoke the language first. Martenns learned it after them."

"I know that already, Desorfk."

"Do you? The elders said you're not keen on studying."

I shrug. Not denying that. "I don't like books."

"But you have an agile form and quick legs. I assume you've practiced running from all those cruel schoolmates?"

I look surprised as he tilts his head with a sympathetic grin. "I'm a goblin. Our kind is hated too. They've tried to steal your blood and put into themselves."

"Yes," I say.

"Brutal. And quite foolish."

"They envy me."

"Any young person would. You're made with extra power."

"But all I can do is breathe fire. I don't know anything else."

Desorfk looks excited as he douses the fire in his shop and starts collecting what look like rusty goblin-crafted weapons. "That's what studying with a mentor is for, Jet."

"So, are we going to see Feuskarg now?"

"Yes. The horses are waiting at the top of the ridge."

"Horses?" I say. I immediately think of Fluri. She could easily carry both of us. "Are you sure there isn't a faster way to get there?"

"Speed is not necessary."

"Why not?"

"Because the first lesson you must learn before meeting the Feurix is how to breathe calm. You talk too fast and too loud."

I watch Desorfk sling a pack over his shoulder as he goes outside and try to contain my enthusiasm by walking slowly behind him. "Do I get any of those weapons?"

"You've got the only weapon you need. Fire."

"Doesn't a Firemartenn train to fight? I need to practice with a sword, Desorfk."

"The only thing you need to practice right now," Desorfk says, "is moving slower." He looks back at me with gleaming eyes. "Step out of line in front of Feuskarg and you'll regret it."

"What will happen?"

"You'll be flame-stormed."

I stop walking. Flame-stormed? By a Feurix? Oh shivs.

4

Into Aeissfaud

"Come, Jet," Desorfk says. "You'll ride Telgra." He circles the two black stallions, reaching up to give them a pat on the nose. "I'll take Magned."

But flying would be better. Way better. Before I can pull myself up onto Telgra's back, Fluri drops from the sky, landing hard in front of us. I know she's insulted just by observing this scene and I'm hoping that her presence will make Desorfk change his mind.

"No," Desorfk says with a calm shake of the head.

"But she's the fastest way there and back!"

"Do you know anything about the Feurix? They'll either kill her or enslave her to the king within a second of spotting us overhead. Feuskarg massacred hundreds of Aludenwolke and you want to bring one of the last straight to him?"

"But..." I look up at Fluri's face, seeing her try to understand the conversation. "But she's strong," I say. "She can fight back if she needs to."

"The she-dragon cannot come." Desorfk hops up onto Magned, looking at the path to Aeissfaud. He went from relaxed to impatient in a short amount of time. "Flying is neither faster nor wiser."

"All right, Deso," I groan. "You win."

"Be careful what you tell her. I understand everything that you say. And don't call me Deso."

Fluri and I quickly exchange whispers before she giggles, looks in Desorfk's direction, then takes off into the sky.

"I heard that," Desorfk says as I mount up.

"No, you didn't."

"My ears are giant funnels. Of course I heard. You called me scat-breath."

"No. I said nohtevit."

"Yes. That's dragonspeak for *scat-breath.*"

"I wish you weren't fluent like me. Makes this less fun."

"So much for a secret conversation, huh?" Desorfk flashes a grin as he steers his horse down the ridge.

"You weren't surprised to see Fluri," I say.

"I wasn't. I know you're planning to fly away with her."

I grip the reins hard, jerking Telgra's head up. He snorts, turning around in a circle. "You've been following me?"

"Does that bother you?"

I've never been this close to the volcanic valley. Smoke, ash, and razor-tipped rocks shadow each step. "No," I say. "I just wonder why you would care. I want to start over somewhere where people actually like me."

"A Firemartenn has the most fragile relationship with society. You won't find as many friends as you think."

"What about the other Martenns? They can be my friends."

"You'll find that out when you meet them."

"And when will I meet them?"

"When they're ready to meet you."

The horses are forced to take small steps forward, unable to predict where the rock will loosen and give way. Parts of the trail are hard as metal, others as unstable as quicksand. Nothing is visible through the ash rain.

"You don't like the idea of me meeting them, do you, Desorfk? You think I'll cause chaos."

"Oh, a Firemartenn always causes chaos. It's part of your personality."

"Is that good or bad?"

"Depends on who you ask."

"Errhaint," I say. *Indeed.*

The ground is smoldering. It's getting steep again.

"How did you learn dragonspeak so well?" Desorfk asks.

"Well, I listened to dragons talking when I was really young. I could hear them but not see them."

"They were hidden."

"Yes."

"Your vocabulary seems basic, but I'm still impressed."

"My mother hated hearing me speak it in the house. She never said it out loud, but I could read it on her face. She was tortured by it."

"But it's a beautiful language."

"She just hates all dragon things."

"One day she will embrace it. She's scared to lose you."

"I doubt that. She wouldn't mind either way if I disappeared off the edge of Ervenfuge."

"She's worried that you will die the same as your father. I was there on the day of your birth, Jet. The elders refused to go near her because of their disdain for Junilier, and I was the second person to receive news of his death. He died only minutes after your birth. Failed to reach the sacred sapphire."

"Forever cursing us both," I sigh. "I was born into his failure."

"No." Desorfk halts his horse and turns to face me. "It is not on you, Firemartenn. Your father did his best."

"And how do you know that? You didn't see his life end."

"I was told everything about it. Every terrible detail."

"By who?"

"His Kamerwalf."

I sit frozen atop Telgra, confused as Desorfk rides on. "His what?"

"A Kamerwalf is the most important thing in a Martenn's life. There's a lot to say about it."

"And? We're going to take forever at this pace. Tell me about it."

"A Kamerwalf is a Martenn's bodyguard. They are born with the duty already set in their heart but won't even know it themselves until something calls them into service."

"And what calls them?"

Desorfk rides to the top of another ridge and waits for me to join him. The weight of magma underground and the pressure of its inner wrath makes Aeissfaud feel alive. Gaseous veils separate us and the valley floor. "When a Martenn is about to die, the Kamerwalf comes to their aid. It's an invisible bond between the two souls."

"So, my father's Kamerwalf couldn't save him?"

"She was mortally wounded during the fight. She shouldn't have even had the strength to get home, but she did. Died on the floor of my shop after telling me what happened to your father."

"Who was she?"

Desorfk lowers his eyes, fiddling with a hunting knife. "My wife."

I watch him peer through the gases. He's fighting to see the volcanoes with his watery orange eyes. "A goblin?" I ask.

"Yes."

"I'm sorry."

"Doesn't matter," he says. "She did what she had to do. We knew what could happen."

"I guess my mother has a reason to be upset. But I really don't think I'll have a problem with the Feurix."

"That's a dangerous mindset to have, Jet. Pride is what got your father killed."

"I'm not proud. Just confident." And confidence is a good trait. I've survived this long in the world because of it.

Out of nowhere, Desorfk gives me a mischievous look and urges Magned into a gallop down the vertical descent.

"Hey! I thought we were going slow!" I follow, trying to match his speed on Telgra. "Desorfk!"

The bottom of the valley is boiling hot. Hotter than I've ever felt. The darkness has swallowed everything around me, and I can't figure out which direction to go. A maze without walls. Thick, stifling air.

"Desorfk!" My chest and throat are tightening. "Where are you, goblin?" I try to yell. But I cough instead, pulling back too hard on Telgra's reins, and he rears, throwing me to the ground.

"Jet?"

I'm dizzy. I can't catch my breath. It's just like when Dymraus was trying to steal my blood. It's the same feeling.

"Your breathing is rapid, Jet." Desorfk's still sitting on his horse. He's looking down at me. "What's wrong with you?"

My heart is pounding. I'm shaking like I did when I was bound to the ehreleit. I can't stop the convulsions. It's uncontrollable.

"Jet!"

I'm sprawled on the scalding ground, a burning pain like I've never felt shooting through my body. It hurts. Why does it hurt like this? I'm not supposed to feel pain. I'm not supposed to feel fire. I am the fire.

5

Questions

"Your breathing is too fast. Slow it down."

"I'm fine, Desorfk."

He watches me roll to my knees. "You're weak."

"It's just convulsions," I say, standing up. "Started after the firestorm that I caused." I don't tell him about the unnatural pain that I felt coursing through me.

"How often does this happen?" he asks.

"Maybe a few times a week. I always recover."

"The Feurix will not go easy on you."

"I'm not afraid of them," I say. I push hair out of my eyes, seeing one of my arms still trembling.

"You are afraid, Jet. Fear weakens the body."

"Eamt nae." *I'm not.*

"You're shaking."

"I have to do this, Desorfk. I want to."

He whistles, sending his horse away from us, and pulls out a vial from behind his back. "Then you need to relax."

"I'm fine."

"Pure lava helps a Firemartenn's nerves."

I take the vial and study the thick liquid inside it. "Did my father drink this?"

"He did. Never had the shakes like you though."

"I'm fine, Deso."

"Drink it."

The lava is numbing as it goes down. It's comforting to not feel a harsh burn.

"Listen, Jet, it's only going to get tougher from here. We have to reach Irakkitide's base within the hour. One way or another, the water must be restored to Ateinekus."

I watch him walk away, taking a minute to realize what he just said. "Water? This whole thing is about water?"

"Retrieving Ackellhnn's sapphire is how we save your kin. A new river will birth from Otrusc's Dome once it's done."

"My kin doesn't care if I live or die."

"No?" Desorfk turns, walking backward as I follow. The air is sizzling from the surrounding volcanic activity. "Your beloved Fluri will die without water too."

"Not if I leave with her."

"You are supposed to defend your birthplace. It's one of the many Martenn duties."

Many duties. Great. I'm bound to serve those who think I shouldn't be alive.

"Jet, the water source affects all of Western Ervenfuge. Your father had more time on his hands when he accepted the task, and he was much more mature. It's your turn now to pick up where he left off. And unfortunately, your youth works against you."

"Why did you send for me if I'm too young?"

"Because we're running out of time. The Feurix will eventually need water too, and they are trying to bring down everyone with them. Part of a selfish nature."

"So the Feurix hide the sapphire because they want to see us all dead?"

"They are waiting for Junilier's progeny." Desorfk looks at the ground, bending down to pick up an obsidian stone. "Everything you do in front of their eyes is a test to see if you have the strength to be their leader."

"But they have a leader. Feuskarg."

"A king does not equal a leader." He starts throwing stones in the air, juggling them without taking his eyes off me. "Half of your heart is in the world of Elves and Ateinekus, half is in the Feurix world. But he will try to turn you against your village. A Martenn must always remain neutral."

I'm slightly annoyed at his playing with rocks while we discuss serious matters. Maybe it's just a strange goblin habit. "Are the Feurix easy to talk to?" I ask, turning away from the distracting juggling act.

"I've never communicated with them," he says. "They only speak with each other and the Firemartenn. And seeing as how you like asking so many questions, your first encounter with Feuskarg may be quite difficult."

"Why? You said that I share their blood."

"The Feurix dislike questions. They are the most temperamental of the dragon breeds."

"You think I'm gonna get fire-stormed from the first word I say."

"I'm only trying to prepare you. And you've never studied well in school…real luck is needed."

"I don't want luck," I say. "I want them to accept me."

Desorfk grips six stones in his hands, staring intently from them to me. He sets them down in the dirt and says to me,

"Jhetsam, look up."

I tilt my head back, staring at the magnificent height of the volcano. "Irakkitide," I breathe.

"The largest of the eight fire mountains. From what I know of Junilier's journey, Firemartenn, this is where our paths part. Go into the tunnel and you will find the Feurix on your own."

"That's it?"

"You and I will have a chance to meet again. That's as long as you stay alive for the first night."

"And just like that you're trusting me to not mess it up in there?"

"I told you, Jet. I'm not your mentor." He nods up at the rim of Irakkitide. "Feuskarg is."

I can tell by Desorfk's body language that he's getting tired of answering questions. He points with his eyes to a tunnel that looks no bigger than a lava hare burrow. And when I step forward, dropping to one knee to find my path inside, he grips my shoulder with a gnarled hand. "Last bit of advice, Jet."

"What?"

"Mirror their movements as a sign of respect. Don't mention your bond with Fluri or he will use it against you. And should Feuskarg allow you to ride one of the Feurix, there's a secret to maintaining balance on their back."

"Which is?"

"A Firemartenn's legs fuse to a Feurix's body so that you can't fall. Usually you ride one standing up."

"How is the flight compared to an Aludenwolke?"

"You'll be dizzy long after the ride."

"And how do I jump off if my legs are fused to it?"

"It's up to the Feurix to drop you."

"What if I'm upside down over a sharp bed of rocks?"

"It takes building respect and trust. Both ways, Jet. You learn from them and they learn from you."

"But what if I'm plummeting to my death?"

"Make use of your fire breath." Desorfk grins, looking entertained at the thought of me falling out of the sky. "You'll figure it out, Firemartenn."

6

Feuskarg

I crawl through the tunnel, surrounded by darkness and heavy volcanic fumes. I don't hear any sound except for my own breathing. No dragon voices.

"Where are you, Feuskarg?" I whisper.

The tunnel begins to widen and the ground shimmers. A smooth obsidian floor. I slowly stand up.

"Kidenhyi, ruhmachta, ihidtyun." A column of blue flame is speaking to me. I pause to listen as the words repeat. "Kidenhyi, ruhmachta, ihidtyun." *Humility, respect, silence.* The flame flickers and weaves around the magma chamber before transforming into a Feurix. He is ten times bigger than Fluri, his voice so loud it rumbles like an endless earthquake. Eyes the color of slate. I feel like a fragile spider looking up into his face. I'm at his mercy.

"Eamt Jet." *I'm Jet.*

"Sohni I Junilier," he says. *Son of Junilier.*

"Ay." *Yes.*

"Eamt Feuskarg. Ea mosz etss, einalkyv Feurixmaratgnn, lue suchopni neichadu ahnx lurr vaahd." *I'm Feuskarg. I must say, little Firemartenn, you look nothing like your father.*

I want to ask if that's a good or bad thing, but I also don't want to risk a rain of fire on my head.

"Lo juedh. Viunh etys," Feuskarg says. *So young. Shifting eyes.* "Ilynn aidtya." *Nervous breath.*

"Ea lurtd karaan eamt hayn." *I can't believe I'm here.*

My body is withstanding the poisonous gases and heat that would kill anyone else. The walls emit small white and blue sparks that sting when they bounce off my skin. Blue fire is the hottest, even for the Firemartenn, and the sensation of it is akin to a double lightning strike.

"Lurrk lo einalkyv, feurix enakay." *You're so little, fire moppet.*

"Ea kentz. Ea asiiut riv." *I know. I hate it.*

"Lue wil raasni sarftiialu." *You will grow stronger.*

Fear and anticipation are about to explode inside of me. I don't want to be afraid of anything. But the Feurix king is much fiercer than I thought he would be. How in the world am I supposed to control a dragon like him? How am I to gain his trust?

"Unvasch mehii, mlae ivandilv." *Teach me, my mentor.* I lower my head, hoping to look respectful. It's strange to not ask questions, but I don't want to get on his bad side.

"Jet Jhetsam," Feuskarg says loudly. He flaps his enormous wings, the sound of sparks echoing in the hollow chamber. A rainbow of flame glows throughout different parts of his body, his core layer of scales appearing as basalt and rhyolite. "Syatre mlae kardn." *Meet my clan.*

I take a deep breath before looking up. The chamber fills with nine other Feurix, all the same size as their king. There shouldn't be room for all of them in here... it's as if the volcano is alive and expanding.

The thought suddenly occurs to me that should Irakkitide erupt, I might end up blasted through the rock, my entire body swallowed by an ocean of liquid fire. I'd probably survive it given my Feurix blood… but who would want to experience being violently thrown in an out-of-control spin in boiling lava? The landing would not be pretty.

"Zey I lue," I say. *Ten of you.*

"Traap scha mehrr. Ulka wil eischa lue tolgaan ceansa tun uaytt caumeras." *There are more. We will show you tunnels leading to other chambers.*

The Feurix move around me like serpents floating in air. They each manifest fire and lava in a different way on their bodies. Some have claws that look like pumice. Some have andesite scales. All are shrouded in a glowing orb of fire, as if they are just an illusion, brought about by a magical spell. But there is no magic here. Dragons are born with these magnificent traits.

"Ea khoauch tun chahren fali lue," I say. *I want to learn from you.*

Feuskarg swings his tail to the left, nodding for two of his clan to come forward. I stare up at the three of them. "Zeigt ulkatt," he says. *Show us.*

"Avlai." *Okay.* Show them what? I hear the growling of the Feurix around me, wondering what I'm doing wrong.

"Feurix aidtya ivv nae lurr silamacht. Maratgnns lurnh sdechna tun feinli silamacht qelsnid. Sdechna tun feurix. Lehfmodae riv wraichdt lue khoauch riv tun edni." *Fire breath is not your power. Martenns can speak to their power source. Speak to fire. Command it where you want it to go.*

This news from Feuskarg throws me off balance. I can do more than breathe fire? I can make it move? I'm confused and shocked and I can't help but say, "Kakyet?" *What?*

The Feurix whip their heads back, snorting flame in response to my question. Just one word spoken in the wrong way and I'm about to be scorched to ash. I duck, covering my head with my arms.

"Feuskarg," one of them barks. "Irakkitide wil vitslei hidd." *Irakkitide will handle him.*

I look up at the Feurix with the cinder nose and amber eyes. The glowing scales on his back stick up like spikes. His voice is deeper than Feuskarg's, but there's a musical tone to it. Like a drumbeat.

"Avlai, Devosiix. Lue ak Brennovk nehebr hidd." *Okay, Devosiix. You and Brennovk take him.*

Devosiix. Devosiix and Brennovk. I grin at my Feurix brothers, thankful that one of them is already sticking up for me.

"Komm, Feurixmaratgnn!" they call out, flying like hurtling arrows into a wide magma tunnel.

I walk hesitantly past Feuskarg, seeing him motion with his head for me to follow the group. After I pass him, I move into a run, wishing so badly that I had been born with massive wings and a tail. Not very impressive, am I, Feurix king?

7

Fire Tag

We're in an even bigger chamber with a granite floor. I have no idea what the rules of the game are, but from what I can gather by watching the Feurix, fire tag means being tagged by a free-floating fireball and then using your own fireball to tag them back. But their methods of circular upside down flying with claws out, coupled with the aggressive whipping of their tails, makes it look like an acceptable form of beating each other up.

I sprint across the floor, rushing to avoid the current path of the dagger-shaped fireball that Brennovk snorted into existence. Now there are four separate fireballs floating in the chamber.

"Heid newrud kentz fer ascey lehfmodae. Tunn juedh." *He wouldn't know the sacred command. Too young.*

"Heid caedli kentz riv." *He could know it.*

I look over my shoulder at Feuskarg and the red and white scaled Feurix beside him. They're observing the game from a distance, their hulking forms casting shadows against the orange walls. They're talking about me.

"Nae," Feuskarg says. "Ea newra chufuel riv." *I would feel it.*

"Ulka scha sokrei tun unvasch hidd." *We are safe to teach him.* "Ay."

They look back at me, smoke rising out of their nostrils as they breathe heavy. They knew I would hear them… so why the dirty looks? And the sacred command… is this the same command that Fluri spoke of when we first met?

"Tarzi fer igies, feurix enakay," Feuskarg says. *Play the game, fire moppet.* "Edni." *Go.*

"Ea daet kentz air." *I don't know how.*

"Sdechna tun fer feurix. Beusha riv tun lurr egniki." *Speak to the fire. Move it to your opponents.*

He wants me to control the fire, but I don't know anything other than breathing it out. I can't make the fire move.

"Skurd mehii." *Watch me.* Feuskarg breathes out a purple fireball and says, "lehtyat." The fireball turns left, floating down the tunnel until he says, "larne homdi!" *Fast around!* And it turns back toward us, changing into an arrow-shaped flame. "Autz lue dai riv." *Now you do it.*

"Ea lurtd." *I can't.*

"Lehfmodae lurr feurix, Jet." *Command your fire.*

Looking around at the Feurix staring at me, I tilt my head back and breathe out a flame. The orange wisp hovers in the air when I run out of breath. I walk beside it, shocked at seeing my own flame in this quiet, calm state.

"Ahnj ivvta riv ednibahn uasi?" *Why isn't it going out?*

"Irakkitide tanne fer Feurixmaratgnn sarftii," Brennovk says. *Irakkitide gives the Firemartenn strength.* "Lurrk ian kondta." *You're in control.*

Wow. I can play with fire. I hold up my hand, reaching to touch the flame, and I put my arm through it, feeling a gentle warmth. "Avlai, feurix," I say confidently. *Okay, fire.* "Kradhet!"

Circle!

Nothing happens.

"Kradhet! Chiesa!" *Circle! Spin!*

Feuskarg exits the chamber as I continue yelling at the flame. The other Feurix return to their game of fire tag, leaving me to figure this out on my own. I feel anger build inside me as I stare at it. Sweat and ash mingle in the locks of hair that I push out of my eyes. If the Feurix say I can command fire, then I have to prove them right.

"Austa hokumnate," I whisper. *Rise higher.* "Hokumnud." *High.* I close my eyes and drop my arms to my sides. I do what Desorfk told me to do… move slow, breathe calm. "Edni tun Devosiix. Autz." *Go to Devosiix. Now.*

Within a minute I hear their voices from the other end of the chamber, all of them chanting my name. "Fer Feurixmaratgnn's ian fer igies. Stil hidd zurchs!" *The Firemartenn's in the game. Tag him back!*

I see them flying toward me in a vortex of orange and blue smoke and instinctively breathe out another flame that shapes itself into a sphere. This time I send it charging toward them with a single word. "Scealix." *Attack.*

No part of me believes I could control a whole firestorm… like the one I brought onto Ateinekus. But as I interact with the Feurix in our rule-bending game underground, I realize that the training ahead is not just about me… but controlling their fire as well as mine.

"Wevtas scha silamacht, Jet," Brennovk says. *Words are power, Jet.* "Autz zeigt ulka lurr eclassehn ittod." *Now show us your resolute side.*

"Air dai ea dai vate?" *How do I do that?*

"Ansefli ian ah knidachya fidlau." *Stand in a pyroclastic flow.*

* * *

I wait at the base of Irakkitide, wondering how anyone could predict such a massive eruption. The gases and lava will come toward me as fast as a Feurix, and I don't know if I'll be able to stand. The force of it will be rib-cracking and brain-melting. The only way I'm surviving is with my Feurix blood.

I look up as blocks of rock spew into the air, watching them explode into hundreds of pieces across Aeissfaud. Desorfk is out there somewhere. Maybe he's watching me.

"Ruhgeiltaas! Ruhgeiltaas, Feurixmaratgnn!" Feuskarg calls down to me. *Steady. Steady.* But his voice is immediately drowned out by the roaring plume of gases and melted rock. I don't draw a breath. My vision tunnels. All I can feel is pain. Skin stripping off my body. All my clothes disintegrate as if I was underwater. I can't stand the burning in my eyes and I fight to lift my arms, yelling in the effort. When is this going to stop?

"Anrae ansefli! Ansefli!" *Keep standing! Stand!*

But I fall. I fall hard.

* * *

I open my eyes to a pitch-black sky. I'm lying in a pile of ash and embers. Half my skin is melted off my body.

"Mutda tlya," Feuskarg says above me. *Nice try.*

I'm alive. But everything burns. Everything hurts so badly that it takes my breath away. Finding out I still have hair on my head makes me laugh. I hear my laughter change to a gasp as I clutch at my ribs, broken and bruised judging by the shooting pain I feel through my abdomen and chest.

"Lue wil lecga larne," he says. *You will heal fast.* "Lue ansse fetri udt efo mitlaes." *You stood firm for ten minutes.*

"Ea aufivned riv fali warfkarntu." *I stopped it from erupting.*

"Nae. Ben lue eavaod fer vlukni. Lue delka nae hegti." *No. But you faced the surge. You did not run.*

"Riv tudhai lo essyi. Fer Feurixmaratgnn sulviraok chufuel merta fali feurix." *It hurts so bad. The Firemartenn shouldn't feel pain from fire.*

"Angsteich cadyun merta. Lue waln ansgati feint ak lue scha ansgati autz." *Fear creates pain. You were afraid then and you are afraid now.*

I roll to my stomach, looking around the valley, wishing I could see my goblin friend run toward me. "Desorfk."

"Lue wil eivetni mitk hidd ian fer sonndasna," Brennovk says. *You will reunite with him in the morning.* "Komm."

Before I stand to follow him, I realize that I've barely got any fabric covering myself. I hope they have new clothes for me too.

8

Riding Zerseltud

"Feurix yedaum slepma, einalkyv Feurixmaratgnn," Brennovk says as we walk together across an obsidian and feldspar striped floor. *Feurix hardly sleep, little Firemartenn.* I fiddle with the itchy collar of my new shirt, disliking how it rests so high on my neck. The Feurix said this warrior-worthy outfit belonged to my father. "Ben wheyta ulka dai slepma, riv ivv untraulite ian magktun." *But when we do sleep, it is submerged in magma.*

His voice is entrancing to listen to, and, given the intense excitement that I've been through today, it almost puts me to sleep. "Bechnox." *Crazy.*

"Getdov aschkeinu. Riv wil maechev riv eingelt udt lue." *Drink cinder wine. It will make it easier for you.*

We pause in the middle of the chamber to study the bright red pool.

"Fer gutief ednita udt ayluvni," he says, looking at my confused face. *The depth goes for leagues.* "Tundevi I ulkatt rovernni fer noknarjae ian traap." *Hundreds of us spend the night in there.*

I just survived a pyroclastic flow that devoured all my clothes and most of my skin, and now, with the urging of my Feurix brothers, I'm expected to sleep it off in a mass of liquid so boiling that it would kill a normal person within seconds.

"Nae merta," I say as I lightly touch the pool's surface. *No pain.* I'm not feeling the true temperature. "Nae overbre." *No burning.*

"Richtu autz lurr cladmenait ivv sarftiialu trav angsteich. Anrae riv vate tuwessi." *Right now your courage is stronger than fear. Keep it that way.*

Once immersed in the magma, I think twice about putting my head under. "Nae angsteich. Nae angsteich," I tell myself. *No fear.* "Allutarweiz ivv avlai." *Everything is okay.*

But the deeper I swim, the thicker the magma grows, and the more my throat tightens. I can't hold my breath like the Feurix. I can't spend all night in boiling magma.

They're all at the bottom in relaxed positions, tails curled around their massive bodies like serene wolf pups. But I sleep in a normal bed at home… and I'm suddenly missing it. I'm Elf too. Not just dragon.

"Avlai!" I announce. *Okay!* "Eamt awlti! Ciedalvrult mehii un lue khoauch ben eamt slepmatach ott refdhu." *I'm out! Flamestorm me if you want but I'm sleeping on rock.*

They don't come after me. The only sound when I reach the surface is the crack and sizzle of magma bubbles. I look around before laying down on the floor and roll to my back. But my eyes won't close. I feel the start of a convulsion and try to stop it by hugging my arms to my chest. This is going to be a long night.

* * *

The next voice I hear above me is Devosiix. He and Brennovk

are arguing, their volume so loud it brings chunks of ceiling down and I barely move fast enough to avoid getting hit by the rock debris. "Zerseltud ivv fer larnegsa Feurix livkhyn!" *Zerseltud is the fastest Feurix alive!*

"Nae. Ea ad!" *No. I am!*

"Heid eyhi tun tayava fer larnegsa I ulkatt!" *He has to ride the fastest of us!*

"Ay. Mehii." *Yes. Me.*

"Brennovk, lue veryai alluta himuai reedatvi! *Brennovk, you lose every sky race!*

I stand, watching the two of them head-butt each other in between bragging and hurling insults. There's a third Feurix in the chamber, and I'm assuming it's the one they are talking about. Zerseltud. His scales resemble jagged shards of white glass. The flame enshrouding his form is black, dim sparks circling his triangle wings as he keeps his head ducked, his glowing amber eyes fixed on me. He looks like the manifestation of a starless night.

"Zurchs andi," Zerseltud growls to Devosiix and Brennovk. *Back away.* "Ea hoschir. Ea hoschir Feurixmaratgnn." *I fly. I fly Firemartenn.*

I notice that his sentences are shorter, almost childlike.

"Jet," Feuskarg says. He steps into view, his kingly presence silencing everyone. "Luidn ivv Zerseltud. Heid uvyzatta aus scealix fali eimdi, ben fernlat denzhiaodi hidd vimmbantei." *This is Zerseltud. He survived an attack from humans, but they damaged his vocal cords.*

"Mosz hav edmeni ah dliyab eidtaen iha," I say. *Must have been a long time ago.* I can't imagine what it was like for people to see the Feurix freely roaming Ervenfuge.

"Dliyab, dliyab eidtaen. Eimdichelot scarmeki scha fer otdlan zhukneil vate lurnh smerkblikt awekerdh ulkatt. Denkrunah vate wheyta lurrk verkitanta ian aitibed, feurix enakay." *Long, long time. Human-forged swords are the only weapon that can mortally wound us. Remember that when you're defending us in battle, fire moppet.*

"Ea wil." *I will.*

"Eyavdii Zerseltud ivv lurr neiva tachvy. Lue mosz ceant hidd." *Riding Zerseltud is your next test. You must lead him.*

Silver horns curved back on Zerseltud's head. The sight of him beside all the others gives me chills.

"Lue wil tayava hidd udt anu dliyab anu lue lurnh," Feuskarg says. *You will ride him for as long as you can.*

Zerseltud snarls at my approach, and I hear Feuskarg chuckle mischievously behind me. I know I'm in for a crazy ride. "Majty lue wil enavhi ki lurr kobbdi daulav ott fer bodlya." *Maybe you will even see your goblin friend on the ground.*

"Nae danlah," I say. *No problem.* "Ea lurnh vitslei luidn." *I can handle this.* I silently count my breaths as I climb onto Zerseltud's back, standing tall instead of sitting down. He shifts beneath me like a rolling wave, huffing a ball of smoke into the air.

"Lurrk ah nezfrem tun dachbrive eyavdii," Feuskarg says. *You're a stranger to dragon riding.*

My mind immediately goes to Fluri and I have to force myself to ignore the thought of us together in the clouds. The Feurix can't know. They'll hurt her.

"Feint vorbeita tun veryai lurr deistak, feurix enakay." *Then prepare to lose your mind, fire moppet.* Feuskarg suddenly utters a dragonspeak word that I don't recognize, and in one body-thrashing motion, Zerseltud shoots through the tunnel, high above Aeissfaud, higher than Fluri ever dared to take me.

I feel like I'm not in my own body. The rush of every sensation and emotion pushes me to stop thinking of anything other than-

Beyond Fluri.

Beyond the village life.

Beyond the adventures I've had in my head.

And we're only gaining speed.

"Whoa! Langkeit, Zerseltud!" I shout. "Langkeit!" *Slow!*

"Nae langkeit. Larne!" He dives with his wings tucked at his sides. We're free-falling from a height I can't fathom.

"Zerseltud, whoa!"

There's no pattern or rhythm in the motion. It's aimless, carefree, completely wild. Directionless. Just like fire. We are a firestorm in the sky.

"Leidti mitk hidd! Aidyat fer samleya anu hidd!" *Lean with him! Breathe the same as him!*

Standing on Zerseltud's back as he drops upside down, I respond to the group of Feurix flying next to us, "Ea lurnh bondiile aidyat veh aky!" *I can barely breathe at all!*

They laugh and spin to the right, leaving several trails of colorful flame in their wake.

Riding Zerseltud is nothing like riding Fluri. He has a dizzying serpentine movement, almost like we're swimming in an angry sea. But we're in the air. Air layered with thick volcanic fumes. He cuts through every turn with his razor-edged wings, continuing to build speed in a manner that creates a firenado. My feet are fused to him as Desorfk said they would be, giving some small comfort that I won't easily fall off. But I can't even see a league ahead of us as we twist through pillars of steam and smoke.

"Tvedul besuttji?" Zerseltud asks. *Still conscious?*

"Ay," I call back.

He pushes himself into a higher speed, sending us straight down into the eye of the firenado. I think he wants me to pass out, but I fight the nausea and dizziness. If I can handle Fluri's air antics, I should handle this Feurix. But he doesn't let up. There's no resting. He could fly this hard forever.

"Celu mitk Feurix," he says. *One with Feurix.* "Celu mitk Zerseltud." *One with Zerseltud.*

For a split second I feel completely bound to him… as if I was the one with wings. As if I was the one carrying all the power. My arms stretch out in the hot wind, my sooty hair flying around my face. I'm part of them. I'm a dragon too.

"Ceant!" Feuskarg yells next to us. *Lead!* "Ceant! Ehrzti hidd wraichdt tun edni!" *Lead! Tell him where to go!*

It hits me that I'm not really in control. None of the Feurix trust me to take charge. Zerseltud is whipping me around in the sky like a baby deer in a bear's jaws.

"Feurixmaratgnn, lue ceant! Lehfmodae hidd!" *Firemartenn, you lead! Command him!*

"Heid ivv nae shavnnikai!" *He is not listening!*

"Heid shavnni. Heid jenlu kadkai tun dai fer gerrhsat." *He listens. He just likes to do the opposite.*

"Zerseltud, lehtyat! Autz!" *Left! Now!*

But Zerseltud flips upside down instead. We fly close to the other volcanoes, dipping parallel to their slopes, and I cough as we are caught up in a mist of orange and purple lava.

"Fanrux!" I yell. *Down!* "Onndi!" *Drop!*

And he drops me. I'm grasping nothing but air as he releases me from our fire bond. Falling.

"Jet, feurix aidtya!" Brennovk shouts.

At the last second I breathe out my fire, slowing my descent, and a dragon claw grips my leg. Brennovk drops me to the ground before landing in front of me. We trade surprised looks and he grins with glimmering eyes. "Sokregen fer Feurixmaratgnn. Lue newra hav bochrak lurr darter." *Saved the Firemartenn. You would have broken your back.*

Thanks, I think. I can't slow my breath. "Ea breaha ah uintir. Ehrzti mehii ea aiv ah uintir." *I need a break. Tell me I get a break.*

He bobs his head, looking to the left of us. "Lurr kobbdi ruvchtdin. Enoutu vate klegar." *Your goblin friend. Over that ridge.*

"Feuskarg," I whisper in a worried voice.

"Daet volgne. Ulka wil mipriuv lue zurchs wheyta riv ivv eidtaen." *Don't worry. We will bring you back when it is time.*

I feel like collapsing as I make the trek toward Desorfk. My legs are wobbly and my vision is blurred. I can't tell if Feuskarg has his eyes on me or not, but if Brennovk is allowing me to walk away, then I'm certain I can go.

How much of this is training? How much of this is playing tricks on the Firemartenn? I've never felt so confused in who I should trust. And I have yet to bring up the sapphire. How in the world am I supposed to get the Feurix to tell me where it is?

9

The Cairns

Desorfk wordlessly hands me a cup of cinder wine.

"What have you been doing this whole time?" I ask him. But I don't know why I even bother with the question since evidence of his activity is right in front of my eyes.

Stacks of rocks, large and small, are everywhere. Some stacks form animal shapes, others look like letters and numbers. "What is this?"

"Cairns."

Cairns. Is he going to make me build them too? But I sit down with my drink and take a sip, hoping we can just ignore the rocks.

"So," Desorfk says, "do you feel any different?"

"I'm sore."

"You look like you're healing quickly."

"Did you see me standing against Irakkitide?"

"No. But I heard it."

"Was I screaming?"

"Didn't hear your voice. But I imagine you looked half-dead in the flow."

I lean back against a large rock, catching a piece of raw mountain pheasant from Desorfk. "I felt more dragon than Elf by the time it was over."

"That's good."

"I've been talking with them. Haven't mentioned the sapphire yet."

"You won't have to." Desorfk looks down as he sorts a pile of red stones. "They will show it to you on their own."

"Why would they do that?"

"Because you're playing their games. Showing off the sapphire is just another act of mischief."

"Mischief," I echo.

"Indeed." He points to a cairn twelve stones tall. "Try taking one from the middle without letting it fall."

"What for?"

"Your breathing is still erratic, Jet. You need to slow your movements."

"No." I shake my head and scoot away from him. "I'm fine."

"The training is not over. They will keep testing you."

"And how will cairns help me?"

Desorfk sits back, gesturing with both hands to the stacks around us. "Stand up and look carefully at each one. Do not rush your eyes."

All right. What's the goblin getting at now? I sigh and get up to look at the layout of stones.

"Don't just stop at one. Observe them all. Maintain the balance."

"Maintain balance of what?"

"Use the calmness of the cairns to calm yourself. Think."

"Deso, what am I supposed to see? It's just a bunch of rocks."

"Wait," he says. "Look at the cairns as a single unit."

I pace back and forth, having no idea of what Desorfk expects me to do here.

"Want more meat?"

"Yes," I say. "Throw it."

He looks up from his place on the ground and smiles as he tosses more raw meat to me. "You like it best that way, don't you?"

"Always," I say. "It's why I like hunting for my own dinner."

"Same. Animal instinct."

As I study a stack of obsidian stones, I notice that it's leaning to one side, and I find myself leaning with it. The stones fall and land in a pattern that looks like a row of letters: L-E-S-D-R-A. I look back at Desorfk to see if he notices it, but he's drawing with a stick in the dirt. I look back at the letters but they are gone.

"Feuskarg mentioned the sacred command," I say.

"I know. He's obsessed with it. So am I."

"Why would you care about it?"

"Because the Firemartenn is the only one who can speak it. And when he does, there's no going back from that destruction."

"Is the command a spell?"

"No. It's a call to rise. For all dragons to return to the surface."

"And it's a bad thing?"

"It's bad for anyone who isn't a dragon."

"And only a Firemartenn can say it?" I kneel in front of a stone pile and play with it, trying to stack my own cairn.

"You're too young to lead an army of Feurix," Desorfk says. "If the dragons aren't calmly controlled…"

"Do the Feurix expect me to say it?"

"No. Feuskarg doesn't want you to say the command."

"Why not?"

"Because it unites all dragons. Feurix want to rule the skies alone. "

I grin as I look at him. "They're not good at teamwork."

"Neither are you. I don't really want you to say the command either."

"Did my father say it?"

"No. He was afraid of the consequences. That was what his Kamerwalf told me."

"What consequences? How bad are we talking?"

Desorfk adds a pumice stone to my cairn. He steadies it with one hand as I balance two more. "You will have to find a way to unify the dragons and the people of Ervenfuge. It may take centuries but it must be done."

"But they will never get along."

"You and the other Martenns are the generation who will change everything."

"Why us?"

The ground rumbles from an eruption, and we both look back at the volcanoes. All eight of them are awakening.

"You don't know what's coming," Desorfk says. "Your presence quickens the arrival of darkness."

What's coming must be terrible because I hear a crack in Desorfk's usually stoic voice.

"Will I be ready for it?" I ask.

"Words are power," he says softly. "The one word that I can't teach you is the power of all powers." He stares into my eyes while laying stones in the dirt, then gestures for me to look down at his rock formation. Six more letters. C-H-U-I-B-A.

"I've lived in this world for nine thousand years. Rumors of a foreign takeover are getting louder," Desorfk says. "Dangerous forces will soon come to Ervenfuge. People think the dragons are an ugly nuisance, but they have no idea that their freedom depends on their existence."

"A war?"

"You still have much to learn."

"But there will be a war?"

"Prophecy has never lied. The youngest group of Martenns is bound to face the coming threat whether they are prepared or not."

"Well," I say, standing back up, "I wish I could do something other than just breathe fire."

"You'll develop more strength, Jet."

Like commanding fire. I decide not to tell Desorfk what the Feurix taught me, but I'm thinking he already knows. He somehow knows everything.

"Will I get wings?"

"No. You will always have the appearance of a typical Ateinekus Elf."

"But I hate that. I want wings and huge muscles."

"You're lucky you can blend in with society. If you had been born with Oxnumeik blood, you would have a massive tail and legs tripping you up."

"Oxnumeik," I say. "Is that the river dragon?"

"Aye. Each breed has different dragon traits. Since yours are easily hidden, you have the advantage of moving through the country undetected. It's safer."

I'm about to respond when I hear the impatient snort of a dragon. Desorfk's eyes widen as he looks past me.

"He's behind me, isn't he?"

Desorfk nods. He remains seated on the ground, watching Feuskarg smash the cairns with his flaming tail. "Temperamental," he mouths to me.

Shivs. Another test.

10

Running

"Hegti," Feuskarg growls. "Hegti larne." *Run fast.*

I turn around to look up at him, hearing him state the names of the volcanoes: Emaltaide, Anyytane, Ekpslaicre, Diodameht, Wavndairti, Uvdancae, Iltaschenix, Irakkitide.

"Aidyat feurix anu lue spungkerr," he says. *Breathe fire as you jump.* "Caltauri lurrhach enoutu eitahl I esdauv." *Catapult yourself over each of them.*

I look to Desorfk who's now standing up. He presses a charred stick into the dirt, slowly and subtly writing more letters. I read them in my head and turn to start running.

"Pretend Dymraus is chasing you," Desorfk says. "Don't let him catch up!"

I count my breaths, inhaling clouds of ash. Feuskarg is right behind me, snorting flame at my heels. "Emaltaide!" he says.

The smallest of the volcanoes, Emaltaide, is the first one I run toward.

"Ulka scha mitk lue, Jet!" *We are with you, Jet!*

I look to my right and see Brennovk and Devosiix running alongside me.

53

"Spungkerr!" Feuskarg bellows behind us. "Spungkerr!" *Jump!*

I get to the rim of the volcano and falter, almost falling in, completely losing my momentum.

"Agranud! Dai riv agranud!" *Again! Do it again!*

Running is my weakness. It has always been my weakness.

"Lue scha fer Feurixmaratgnn!" Devosiix calls. *You are the Firemartenn!* "Dai riv!"

I turn and go back down the slope to stand at the bottom. I sprint up, this time taking the wild leap to the other side.

Airborne.

No Feurix helping me.

Just myself vaulting across a giant volcanic chasm.

I hit the rim and run down it toward the next one, hearing Feuskarg yelling at me to jump higher. He wants me to breathe fire. But I can barely breathe at all right now. This is beginning to feel like the races in school where I came in last.

Dymraus always knocked me to the ground.

My classmates beat me up for being weak.

The elders would walk by and see me laying there and didn't stand up for me.

I came home with welts and bruises and Mother didn't say a word.

"Ay! Feurix kronvey! Ay!" Devosiix yells.

Suddenly I realize I'm upside down above Wavndairti, the fifth volcano, and holding myself in the air with a strong breath of fire. I'm breathing the fire longer than I've ever done it and it's saving me from plummeting down into the chasm.

"Lurr silamacht raasnis," Feuskarg says to the right of me. *Your power grows.*

I can see him in my upside-down position, and while continuing to breathe out a steady flame, I right myself in the air, touching down on the other side of the volcano's rim. I'm doing it. I'm running and leaping over volcanoes like the Feurix want me to do. But the excitement of using my own fire changes something in my body. It breaks my focus. I sprint down the slope and I feel dizzy.

Aeissfaud is spinning. The ground feels like ocean waves. I can't steady myself. I can't stop the convulsions from coming.

"Hegtikun ivv orhi wetarnei tunn." Feuskarg stares at me as I drop to one knee. *Running is our weakness too.* "Vate ivv ahnj lue tayava ah Feurix." *That is why you ride a Feurix.*

I hold my arms against my chest, struggling to regain the strength that I just had. "Feuskarg," I whisper. I don't know why I'm saying this. I don't know why I'm even going to try. "Feuskarg, zeigt mehii fer safiuvta." *Show me the sapphire.*

His shadow circles me as I look at the ground. "Lue daet khoauch tun sokreg Ateinekus." *You don't want to save Ateinekus.*

I don't belong there. But this is for them. Not for me. "Ea lurtd reuran widhiy fer safiuvta," I say. *I can't return without the sapphire.*

"Lue lurtd hav riv." *You can't have it.*

I keep my head down, watching Feuskarg's claws dig into the hot dirt. I wonder if Desorfk is nearby and secretly listening to the conversation. I feel, at the least, that I should complete this quest for him and his goblin people. They deserve the water.

Lifting my eyes to Feuskarg, I say, "Ea wil dai kakyet mlae vaahd caedli nae." *I will do what my father could not.*

"Feint lue wil embrahe fer Feurix." *Then you will embrace the Feurix.*

"Ea ad ott batrai ittods." *I am on both sides.*

"Lue lurtd bil batrai." Feuskarg breathes hard in my face,

sending dragon saliva all over me. *You can't be both.* "Otdlan celu." *Only one.*

"Ea ad batrai," I say firmly. *I am both.* "Eamt Elf ak drachebrive." *I'm Elf and dragon.*

"Tyadirat davtri fer wulveita." *Fight against the village.*

"Nae." I slowly shake my head. "Ea dae khoauch tun tyadirat anntucelu." *I don't want to fight anyone.*

"Lue dai nae cartag casmarea." *You do not carry peace.*

I'm frustrated with you, Feuskarg. "Fer safiuvta." *The sapphire.*

"Nae."

"Ea wil dai anntuweiz." I push myself off my knee, standing and looking straight up at his eyes. *I will do anything.*

"Lue wil maechev ah vyiwaat, Jet," he says. *You will make a choice, Jet.*

"Kakyet vyiwaat?" I whisper as I follow him back into Irakkitide's tunnels. *What choice?*

His voice echoes, collapsing parts of the walls. "Vyiwaat ivv allutarweiz tun ah Maratgnn. Allutarweiz tun fer drachbriven I Ervenfuge." *Choice is everything to a Martenn. Everything to the dragons of Ervenfuge.*

11

Choice

Feuskarg leads me to the edge of the magma pool where we both come to a halt. I peer at him out of the corner of my eye to see him intently looking into the boiling liquid. Turning my attention back to the surface of the pool, I notice a violet color mixed in with the red magma. A chain is attached to the floor. Then I see the eyes inside the pool. Fluri. They have Fluri.

"Oznaiti durarset!" I spit at Feuskarg. *Tricky durarset!* "Mlae Fluri!"

"Aludenwolke trinludt," Zerseltud says. *Aludenwolke drowns.* He walks around me, slamming his tail into my legs. I fall on my back, staring up at the mob of Feurix surrounding me.

"Lozzt heiss edni." *Let her go.*

They say nothing.

"Lozzt heiss edni!" I scream at them until my voice is hoarse. I can do nothing else against them. "Ea lehfmodae lue! Daenatda heiss! Daenatda mlae edelkus autz!" *I command you! Release her! Release my edelkus now!*

The Feurix show no emotion.

"Jet," Brennovk speaks softly. "Ulka kentin Fluri antunlin shal kentin lue." *We knew Fluri before she knew you.*

"Evzunte, Brennovk, lozzt heiss edni." *Please, Brennovk, let her go.*

"Aludenwolke daet leeskai livkhyn." *Aludenwolke don't leave alive.*

"Evzunte! Shavnn tun mehii!" I get to my feet, yelling and gesturing to Fluri in the magma. *Please! Listen to me!* "Lue daet udaeplei! Shal ivv mlae edelkus!" *You don't understand! She is my edelkus!*

Brennovk lowers his head, backing away from me. The others make way for Feuskarg to place himself between me and them.

"Lue vyiwahl, feurix enakay," Feuskarg says. *You choose, fire moppet.*

My jaw drops when he reveals the sapphire. It's been hidden within his obsidian scales this whole time. "Ah ceandae mosz tetzuvi maechev ah vyiwaat." *A leader must always make a choice.*

I look to the pool. Between Fluri and saving Ateinekus…the Feurix know what I would pick. They've always known.

"Nae," I whisper. "Ea lurtd." *I can't.*

"Vate ivv air lue ikazpri lurrhach." *That is how you prove yourself.*

"Nae. Evzunte, Feuskarg. Evzunte daet lozzt Fluri iednek." *Please, don't let Fluri die.*

"Riv ivv einros," Feuskarg says. *It is simple.* He paces the chamber, weaving around the other Feurix as they silently watch us. "Etss fer wetva, Feurixmaratgnn, ak lue sokreg celu. Etss riv." *Say the word, Firemartenn, and you save one. Say it.*

Say the word.

Word.

The command.

I think about the letters that Desorfk spelled out with stones, trying to figure out how the sacred word would sound in my head.

And the final group of letters he had written: E-T-A-I.

It has to be the command. What else would he write in front of me? But he said he doesn't want me to say it.

I look around at the circle of Feurix. Their eyes are glowing in a menacing light. The Feurix don't want me to say it.

I look past them at Fluri in the magma pool. She will die in front of me. She will die if I don't do something. Something more foolish than I've ever done.

"Vyiwahl ulkatt ak lue anrae heiss," Feuskarg says. *Choose us and you keep her.*

One shot. I have one shot at this. I take a deep breath. "Lue," I say. "Anrae fer safiuvta." *Keep the sapphire.*

Feuskarg stands taller, looking proud of himself. He tilts his head toward the pool. "Daenatda fer Aludenwolke." *Release the Aludenwolke.*

I don't move a muscle. I clench my fists to my sides.

Brennovc breaks the chain with his jaws and I watch Fluri climb out of the pool free.

I follow her as she moves to the tunnel's exit, laying a hand on her neck when she looks down at me. She nods at my serious face, knowing what I'm about to do, and lowers herself to the floor for me to climb onto her back. I briefly think about making a quiet exit, flying far from Aeissfaud and Ateinekus and never looking back, but I can't. I was not born for a quiet end.

"Bil orstigna," Fluri whispers. *Be careful.* She's nervously flapping her wings as she stands in place. "Orstigna, Jet."

But a Firemartenn isn't careful.

A Firemartenn is chaos.

"Celu mehrr weiz, Feuskarg," I say. *One more thing, Feuskarg.*

Feuskarg's eyes shift from a smug glow to an angry shadow. He knows what's coming.

"Lesdrachuibaetai." As I breathe out the last syllable, I feel a thunderous tremor beneath me. A surge of energy sends magma splashing in every crevice and tunnel of Irakkitide's core.

I've just awakened every dragon in Ervenfuge.

"Feurix enakay," Feuskarg growls. "Nae!" He rears up, sucking in his breath to fire-storm me and Fluri, but there's no way I'm staying here to get scorched to a crisp.

"Hegti! Hegti, Fluri!" *Run!*

She charges out of the tunnel and into the sky as a swirl of blue flame overcomes my eyes. I can hear Desorfk screaming at me from below. Feurix are pouring out of the volcanoes, their bodies forming one massive wall of wings and fire.

"Jet! Tell her to dive hard left! Left!"

12

The Firemartenn

We're flying low, Fluri wildly veering right and left.

"Anfozlyat!" Desorfk screams. *Desist.* He hurls a poison-dipped spear, and as I duck, I hear a vengeful roar behind me.

"Anfozlyat!" he screams again. His powerful voice doesn't match his little body.

Fluri touches the ground, running alongside Desorfk.

"A Feurix just tried to bite your head off!" Desorfk says. "Get out of here!"

"What can you do to stop them? You're a goblin!"

"I'm not just a goblin, Jet."

I look back to see who is still roaring from the spear attack. It's Zerseltud. His mouth is open and I notice something shiny around his neck. Ackellhnn's sapphire. He has the sapphire.

"I'm a Kamerwalf!" Desorfk shouts, throwing a boulder over his head like it was a pebble. The boulder hits Zerseltud, but it does nothing to harm him.

"My Kamerwalf?"

He has a joyful grin on his face despite being surrounded by angry Feurix. "Your Kamerwalf."

Great timing to announce that. Really. "Where were you when I was almost killed after my honor ceremony?"

"Fluri was there. I knew she would save you."

A spontaneous game of keep-away begins among the Feurix, each of them tossing the sapphire to each other with their teeth until Feuskarg catches it. I wonder why they haven't flown away yet…maybe they won't cause the destruction that Desorfk said they would.

But Desorfk comes back around with the spear he had thrown at Zerseltud and thrusts it at the chain holding the sapphire. The sapphire falls from Feuskarg's neck into his hands and he sprints toward the closest ridge. "Jet!" Desorfk throws the sapphire to me and I catch it in a frantic tumble.

Now I'll be a crispy Elf-dragon for sure because I took the sapphire back. I took it back in a silly little game among fire dragons and a goblin. "All right," I say, closing my eyes. "Get this over with."

But no fire comes. No scathing growl or hiss from the Feurix.

"Jet," Desorfk whispers, "I really wish you hadn't said that word."

"Everything's fine," I say, eyes still closed. "They're calm." I clutch the sapphire to my chest, in disbelief that I'm actually holding it. I don't know what else to do.

"Listen to me. You need to bring the sapphire to Otrusc's Dome. The water is flowing free now, but it must be brought back."

"Are they still staring at me?"

"No." Desorfk sighs. "No, they're-"

I hear distant screams and open my eyes, looking toward Ateinekus. The ashen sky is alight with flame. The Feurix are attacking my home.

"You've no idea what you just started."

"They'll listen," I say. "I'm their leader."

Desorfk jumps up onto Fluri with me, a crossbow at his side. "Protect your family at all costs."

"How do I do that while defending the Feurix?"

"Firemartenn instinct."

"But I don't want to anger Feuskarg more."

"You won't," Desorfk says as he takes in the scene below. "That's my job." He flashes a mischievous grin and lets himself fall backward, landing perfectly onto a galloping horse.

"Wow," I say. "Legendary Kamerwalf."

"Jet, suchopni!" Fluri says. *Look!*

A curtain of blue fire separates us from the village. The Feurix are terrorizing everyone. "Wheyta ea etss fer wetva," I call to Fluri, "kipdai svezkru!" *When I say the word, flip upside down!*

I aim for Feuskarg as I drop, catching the tip of his tail. I run up his back, firmly planting myself between his fiery shoulder blades. "Edni zurchs, Feuskarg!" *Go back!*

Water is flowing out of Otrusc's Dome. A new river emerges near the ehreleit and I've fulfilled my father's oath. But it's not enough. "Pravsn esdauv zurchs! Eamt fer Feurixmaratgnn!" *Send them back! I'm the Firemartenn!*

Feuskarg's ignoring my voice as he continues to blaze houses with his fire breath. I can't tell if other dragon breeds have yet taken to the sky, but there must be thousands of them. Their lives will be at risk from hunters in Ervenfuge.

"Fluri!" I call out as she flies beneath us. "Ehrzti esdauv tun drehtz homdi!" *Tell them to turn around!*

"Fernlat wardhi shavnn!" *They won't listen!*

"Do your job, Firemartenn!" Desorfk screams. He's firing arrows into the sky, trying to distract the Feurix. A few of the elders bring out their own bows to join his worthless efforts.

"Make them listen to you! Make them!"

I yelp as Feuskarg tries to throw me off his back, holding on with every bit of strength that I have.

"Kidenhyi, ruhmachta, ihidtyun." Feuskarg chants the same words he had said when I first met him. He has a weaker tone in his voice. A sadness. "Iuladit!" he cries. *Disloyalty.*

A wave of dizziness hits me and convulsions take my body. I steady my breathing, fearing that I'll be dropped to the ground. But Feuskarg doesn't let me fall. The fire enshrouding his body is flickering just like my limb spasms, and I notice that his breathing is rapid like mine. We breathe together, flying lower to the village.

"You're the same," I whisper.

Feuskarg feels cheated and betrayed. I can sense his anger inside my heart. He is misunderstood the same as me... I'm just like them.

"Eavek ruhgel mitk fer Feurix." *I'll stay with the Feurix.* The shaking stops. My body relaxes. "Eavek zhile ian Irakkitide." *I'll live in Irakkitide.*

"Ulka scha lurr heinay," Feuskarg says. *We are your home.* "Avsalli." *Forever.*

Though he can't see me, I bow my head in a sign of submission. I can never go back to my old life, not anymore.

Desorfk is riding Fluri beside us, and he nods silently, knowing what I have chosen to do. "We'll be behind you," he says. "I'll tell your mother."

Without speaking, Fluri and I understand each other. She will always be my edelkus, but I must live among the Feurix. I must continue to learn my powers.

"Tun heinay!" Feuskarg calls. *To home!* "Tun heinay!" His

voice booms through the crackling of fire.

My back is turned to the village as I stand atop Feuskarg, leading the mass of Feurix back into Aeissfaud. But I hear a faint voice calling my name. "Jet!"

I look over my shoulder and see my mother standing on a ridge with Fluri and Desorfk. She's leaning into the hot wind, hands cupped around her mouth. "Be safe! Be safe, Jet!"

I'm too stunned to say anything as the three of them fade behind me, their silhouettes covered by the volcanic gases, and then there is nothing around me but fire. I sigh, closing my eyes against the swirl of rock and lava. Feuskarg roars, his clan echoing around us.

I have two homes. Two families. My duty is to defend them both.

"Edni tun Zerseltud," Feuskarg says and flips upside down. I land on Zerseltud's tail as we dive into the center of Irakkitide. I stretch out my arms, taking on the force of a blistering magma tsunami, and touch the obsidian floor.

"Feurixmaratgnn," Feuskarg says, "lue hav eiotli tun dai." *You have work to do.*

I look up with a grin, taking in the wild eyes of my mentor. "Eamt gobeir." *I'm ready.*

Let the Feurix games begin.

13

Map And Dragonspeak Pronunciation Guide

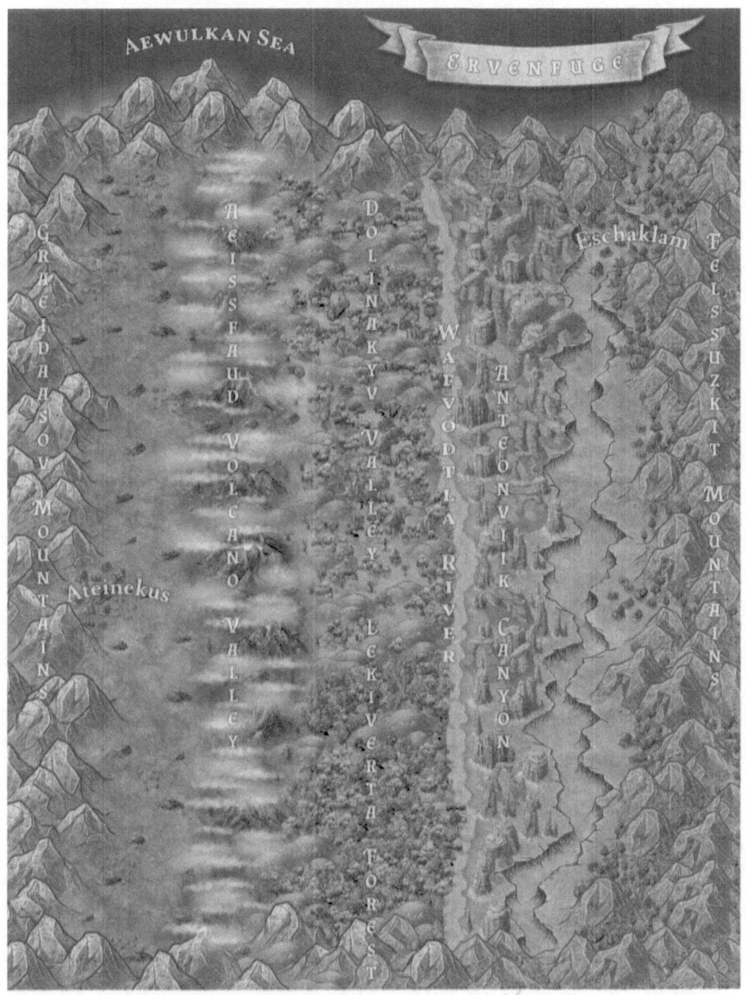

Pronunciation Guide/*Dictionary*

Avlai- Ahv-lye: *Okay*

Ahnx- Ox: *Like*

Ansse- Ans: *Stood*

Aufivned- Ahf-iv-ned: *Stopped*

Angsteich- Ahn-stike: *Fear*
Ansgati- Ans-gotti: *Afraid*
Avsalli- Ahv-sally: *Forever*
Anrae- Ahn-ray: *Keep*
Austa- Ahs-tah: *Rise*
Air: *How*
Anu- Ahn-oo: *As*
Antulin- Ahn-too-lihn: *Before*
Ansefli- An-sehf-lee: *Stand*
Ah: *A*
Anseflim- Ans-eff-lim: *Standing*
Aiv: *Get*
Aivi- Eye-vee: *Getting*
Ay: *Yes*
Ak: *And*
Ascey- Ay-see: *Sacred*
Autz- Ahts: *Now*
Asiiut- As-wit: *Hate*
Aidyat- Eyed-yat: *Breathe*
Aidtya- Eyed-tya: *Breath*
Ahnj- Ahj: *Why*
Aky- Ack-ee: *All*
Allutarweiz- Al-oo-tar-wise: *Everything*
Anntuweiz- Ahn-too-wise: *Anything*
Anntucelu- Ahn-too-sell-oo: *Anyone*
Alluta- Al-oo-tah: *Every*
Aschkeinu- Ash-kay-noo: *Cinder wine*
Aus- Ahs: *An*
Andi- An-dee: *Away*
Ayluvni- Ay-love-nee: *Leagues*
Agranud- Ahg-rahn-ud: *Again*

Aitobed- Eyet-oh-bed: *Battle*
Awekerdh- Awe-kerth: *Wound*
Awlti- All-tee: *Out*
Ad: *Am*
Altashn:- Alt-ash: *Older*
Beel: *Was*
Ben: *But*
Bil: *Be*
Besuttji- Behs-utt-jee: *Conscious*
Bechnox- Beck-nox: *Crazy*
Bochrak- Bok-rack: *Broken*
Bodlya- Bohd-yah: *Ground*
Bondiile- Bond-eel: *Barely*
Batrai- Bah-try: *Both*
Breaha- Bree-ha: *Need*
Beusha- Bo-sha: *Move*
Blakinsok- Blak-in-sock: *Nonsense*
Caltauri- Cahl-tar-ee: *Catapult*
Caedli- Cayd-lee: *Could*
Chiesa- Chee-sah: *Spin*
Cadyun- Cad-yune: *Creates*
Chufuel- Cheh-full: *Feel*
Celu- Sell-oo: *One*
Chahren- Chah-ren: *Learn*
Ceansa- Sin-sah: *Leading*
Ceant- Sinnt: *Lead*
Ceandae- Sin-day: *Leader*
Cladmenait- Clad-mehn-ight: *Courage*
Caumeras- Kom-air-ahs: *Chambers*
Cartag: *Carry*
Casmarea- Cahs-mare-ee: *Peace*

Ciedalvrultin- See-dal-roo-tin: *Flame-stormed*

Dachbriven- Dahk-briv-ehn: *Dragons*

Daenatda- Day-nat-dah: *Release*

Deistak- Day-stack: *Mind*

Dliyab- Lee-ahb: *Long*

Denkrunah- Den-kroo-nuh: *Remember*

Doppvat: *Double*

Denzhiaodi- Dens-ay-oh-dee: *Damaged*

Darter: *Back (the body part)*

Daulav- Dah-lahv: *Friend*

Drehtz: *Turn*

Davtri- Dahv-tree: *Against*

Dai: *Do*

Daet- Date: *Don't*

Durarset- Durr-are-set: *fool/mischief-maker*

Delka: *Did*

Ea- Ee: *I*

Eamt- Eemt: *I'm*

Edelkus- Ehd-ell-kuss: *A beloved person or creature*

Ehreleit- Air-eh-light: *ceremonial platform/rostrum*

Errhaint- Air-haynt: *Indeed*

Embrahe- Ehm-brah-hee: *Embrace*

Etss: *Say*

Einros- Eyen-rose: *Simple*

Etys- Ett-iss: *Eyes*

Egniki- Egg-nick-ee: *Opponents*

Edni- Ed-nee: *Go*

Ednibahn- Ed-nee-bon: *Going*

Evzunte- Ehv-zoon-tay: *Please*

Eclassehn- Eck-lass-enn: *Resolute*

Eavaod- Ee-vod: *Faced*

Essyi- Ess-yee: *Bad*

Enavhi- Ehn-ah-vee: *Even*

Eiotli- Eye-ott-lee: *Work*

Eivetni- Eye-vet-nee: *Reunite*

Eavek- Ee-vek: *I'll*

Enoutu- En-oh-too: *Over*

Eidtaen- Eyed-tane: *Time*

Ehrzti- Airs-tee: *Tell*

Ednita- Ed-nee-tah: *Goes*

Eyhi- Ee-hee: *Has*

Esdauv- Ess-dahv: *Them*

Einaunli- Eye-non-lee: *Amazing*

Edmeni- Ehd-men-ee: *Been*

Eyavdii- Ay-ahv-dee: *Riding*

Eingelt- Eyen-gelt: *Easier*

Einalkyv- Eye-nalk-ivv: *Little*

Enakay- Een-ah-kay: *Moppet*

Eimdi- Aim-dee: *Humans*

Eimdichelot- Aim-dike-el-lot: *Human-forged*

Fali- Fall-ee: *From*

Feurix- Fury: *Fire*

Feurixgrozt- Fury-grote: *Firestorm*

Fernlaty- Fern-lat-ee: *They'll*

Fanruttiln- Fan-roo-tiln: *Underground*

Fer: *The*

Fernlat- Fern-lat: *They*

Fanrux: *Down*

Feinli- Fayn-lee: *Their*

Feint- Faynt: *Then*

Fetri- Feh-tree: *Firm*

Eitahl- Eye-tall: *Each*

Fidlau- Fihd-law: *Flow*

Feurixmaratgnn- Fury-mar-ah-tane: *Firemartenn*

Gutief- Guh-teef: *Depth*

Getdov: *Drink*

Guthost- Gut-ust: *Good*

Gerrhsat- Gar-sat: *Opposite*

Gobeir- Go-beer: *Ready*

Gehanha- Geh-hahn-hah: *Secret*

Hayn: *Here*

Hoschir- Hosh-eer: *Fly (to fly in the sky)*

Homdi- Hom-dee: *Around*

Hidd: *Him*

Heiss- High-ess: *Her*

Heid- Hide: *He*

Hokumnud- Hock-oom-nud: *High*

Hokumnate- Hock-oom-nate: *Higher*

Hegti- Heg-tee: *Run*

Heinay- Heen-ay: *Home*

Hav: *Have*

Himuai- Him-oo-eye: *Sky*

Ivv: *Is*

Ivvta: *Isn't*

Iha- Ee-hah: *Ago*

Ittod: *Side*

Iednek- Eed-nek: *Die*

Imliatt- Ihm-lee-at: *Kill*

Ikdisatz- Ick-dee-sats: *Landing*

Ikazpri- Ick-ahs-pree: *Prove*

I: *Of*

Iuladit- Ill-ad-it: *Disloyalty*

Ian: *In*

Igies- Ihg-eyes: *Game*

Ivandilv- Ihv-an-div: *Mentor*

Ihidtyun- Ee-hid-tyun: *Silence*

Ilynn- Ill-inn: *Nervous*

Juedh- Joo-eth: *Young*

Jenlu- Jehn-loo: *Just*

Kadkai: *Likes (a person's behavior/he or she likes...)*

Klegar- Klay-gahr: *Ridge*

Kobbdi- Kohb-dee: *Goblin*

Kronvey- Kronn-vay: *Blood*

Kakyet- Kahk-yet: *What*

Kakyeti- Kahk-yet-ee: *What's*

Ki- Kee: *See*

Kipdai- Kip-dye: *Flip*

Khoauch- Ko-aush: *Want*

Kentz- *Know*

Karaan- Kar-ahn: *Believe*

Kardn- Kahrd: *Clan*

Kondte- Kon-tay: *Control*

Kradhet- Krath-ett: *Circle*

Knidachya- Nihd-ak-yah: *Pyroclastic*

Kidenhyi- Kidd-ehn-high: *Humility*

Komm: *Come*

Leidti- Lay-tee: *Lean*

Langkeit- Lang-kite: *Slow*

Lue- Loo: *You*

Lurr: *Your*

Lurrk: *You're*

Lo: *So*

Larnegsa- Larn-egg-sah: *Fastest*

Larne- Lahrn: *Fast*

Lurrhach- Lurr-hock: *Yourself*
Leeskai- Lee-sky: *Leave*
Lecga- Lek-gah: *Heal*
Luidn- Loo-ihn: *This*
Lehfmodae- Leff-moh-day: *Command*
Lozzt- Lots: *Let*
Lesdrachuibaetai- Lehs-drahk-oo-beht-eye: *"Dragons To Awake" (Sacred Firemartenn command)*
Lurnh- Lurn: *Can*
Lurtd- Lurt: *Can't*
Lehtyat- Let-yat: *Left*
Livkhyn- Lihv-kin: *Alive*
Mitk- Mikk: *With*
Mehii- Meh-hee: *Me*
Mlae- Mly: *My*
Maechev- Mai-kev: *Make*
Majty- Mayt-tee: *Maybe*
Mosz- Moss: *Must*
Mutda- Mutt-dah: *Nice*
Merta- Merr-tah: *Pain*
Mehrr- Mare: *More*
Magktun- Mag-tunn: *Magma*
Mipriuv- Mee-pree-uhv: *Bring*
Neichadu- Nigh-kah-doo: *Nothing*
Nehebr- Neh-bair: *Take*
Newrud: *Wouldn't*
Newra: *Would*
Neiva- Nay-vah: *Next*
Nezfre: *Stranger*
Nae: *No/Not*
Noknarjae- Nock-are-jai: *Night*

Nohtevit- Not-eh-vit: *Scat-breath (a dragon insult)*
Ottun- *Onto*
Orstigna- Ohr-stig-nah: *Careful*
Overbre- Oh-ver-bray: *Burning*
Overb: *Burn*
Oznaiti- Ohz-nye-tee: *Tricky*
Olsu- Ohl-soo: *Off*
Otdlan- Ott-lahn: *Only*
Ott: *On*
Orhi- Or-hee: *Our*
Onndi- Ohn-dee: *Drop*
Pravsn- Prav-sen: *Send*
Priteag- Pree-tag: *Hello/Greetings*
Qelsnid- Kells-nidd: *Source*
Riv: *It*
Richtu- Rik-too: *Right*
Rufite- Roof-ite: *Call*
Reuran- Roo-rahn: *Return*
Raasni- Rahs-nee: *Grow*
Reedatvi- Reed-aht-vee: *Race*
Rovernni- Rohv-er-nee: *Spend*
Refdhu- Ref-thoo: *Rock*
Ruhgeiltaas- Roo-gill-toss: *Steady/Be Calm*
Ruhgel- Roo-gehl: *Stay*
Scha- Skah: *Are*
Sameilte- Sam-eelt: *Really?*
Slepmatach- Slep-mat-ak: *Sleeping*
Slepma- *Sleep*
Sokrei- Sok-ray: *Safe*
Sarftiiak- Sarf-tee-ak: *Strong*
Sonnkhtja- Sunk-jah: *At sunrise*

Syatre- Sott: *Meet*
Sohni- Sun-hee: *Son*
Scealix- Skee-lix: *Attack*
Stil: *Tag*
Spungkerr- Spun-care: *Jump!*
Samleya- Sam-lee-ah: *Same*
Sonndasha: Sun-dash-ah: *Morning*
Sulviraok- Sull-veer-ok: *Shouldn't*
Scarmeki- Skar-mek-ee: *Swords*
Sdechna- Dehk-nah: *Speak*
Shal: *She*
Smerblikt- Smerr-blik: *Mortally*
Suchopni- Such-up-nee: *Look*
Sarftiialu- Sarf-tee-all-loo: *Stronger*
Sarftii- Sarf-tee: *Strength*
Svezkru- Vez-kroo: *Upside down*
Safiuvta- Sahf-oov-tah: *Sapphire*
Sokregen- Sok-ray-gun: *Saved*
Sokreg- Sok-rehg: *Save*
Schulprivn- Skull-priv-enn: *Owe*
Silamacht- Sill-ah-mock: *Power*
Shavnni- Shavv-nee: *Listens*
Shavnn- Shavv: *Listen*
Shavnnikai- Shavv-neek-eye: *Listening*
Terve: *Hold*
Tvedul- Vehd-ool: *Still*
Tayava- Tay-ah-vah: *Ride*
Tanne- Tan-nay: *Gives*
Tarzi- Tar-see: *Play (to play a game)*
Traap- Trap: *There*
Tun: *To*

Tunn: *Too*

Tyadirat- Tah-deer-aht: *Fight*

Tetzuvi- Teht-zoo-vee: *Always*

Trinludt- Trin-loot: *Drowns*

Tuwessi- Too-wes-see: *Way*

Tolgaan- Toll-gahn: *Tunnels*

Tundevi- Toon-dehv-ee: *Hundreds*

Tudhai- Tuth-eye: *Hurts*

Tachvy- Tack-vee: *Test*

Trav: *Than*

Tlya- Lye-ah: *Try*

Udt- Utt: *For*

Untraulite- Un-trah-light: *Submerged*

Ulka- Ohl-kah: *We*

Ulkatt- Ohl-kat: *Us*

Uaytt- Yott: *Other*

Uvyzatta- Oov-zat-uh: *Survived*

Udaeplei- Ood-eye-plee: *Understand*

Uth- Ooth: *Up*

Un- Oon: *If*

Uintir- Een-teer: *Break*

Unvasch- Uhn-vash: *Teach*

Volgne- Volg-nay: *Worry*

Vorbeita- Vohr-bay-tah: *Prepare*

Vitslei- Vit-sleigh: *Handle*

Votind- Voh-tind: *East*

Vate: *That*

Veh: *At*

Vimmbantei- Vim-bahn-tay: *Vocal cords*

Veryai- Verr-eye: *Lose*

Vyiwaat- Wee-waht: *Choice*

Vyiwahl- Vee-wall: *Choose*
Vlukni- Vlook-nee: *Surge*
Vaahd- Vahd: *Father*
Vaasa- Vah-sah: *Mother*
Viunh- Vee-oon: *Shifting*
Wardhi- War-thee: *Won't*
Wundeircha- Wund-eer-kah: *Beautiful, lovely*
Wheyta- Way-tuh: *When*
Widhiy- With-ee: *Without*
Wetarnei- Wet-are-nay: *Weakness*
Wraichdt- Rayt: *Where*
Wil: *Will*
Weiz- Wise: *Thing*
Wetva: *Word*
Wulveita- Wohl-veet-ah: *Village*
Waln: *Were*
Weilouv- Way-loov: *Because*
Yedaum- Yeh-dahm: *Hardly*
Zurchs: *Back*
Zey- Zay: *Ten*
Zeigt- Zayg: *Show*
Zhile-Zile: *Live*

About the Author

Han M Greenbarg has been in love with writing fiction since childhood. She is an avid coffee drinker, proud dog mom, and lover of country music and war movies. Her biggest jolts of inspiration stem from nature, a variety of film scores, and animals of all kind.

You can connect with me on:
- https://www.hanmgreenbarg.com
- https://www.instagram.com/hanmgreenbargauthor

Also by Han M Greenbarg

Scurts Flightplan

With three months left to live in a stifling, post-nuclear city, Damon Scurto believes he has one last shot at finding the grave of the woman who got away. He is best friends with a guy who eats paper, best frenemies with a convicted killer, and is the bane of his wine-drunk therapist's existence.

Elf Bat Book One Kiah

Twelve years after the ruthless massacre of his parents and most of his kin, eighteen-year-old Elf Bat Kiah lives a life of internalized grief and solitude in his family's cave. The arrival of Fly, a reckless purebred Elf maiden, sparks the flame for revenge and a resurgence of the Bats.

Elf Bat Book Two Sacrifice

The revenge of the Elf Bats has begun in Sidhovvn, each Bat warrior facing down the count who carried out the ruthless slaughter of their family. But in the midst of seeking justice against the purebred king and his soldiers, the sudden emergence of Fly's demon-driven adoptive mother Ixetmori proves to be the bigger test of wills, and the defining moment of what it means to be courageous.

Chehnuh

Year 2018. Chehnuh, a half-elven and sole survivor of his people's genocide, resides quietly in a remote cabin in the Sierra Nevada mountains. No one knows how he came to the United States. No one knows that he is part Elf. He is a mystery to all who meet him until a young widowed mother interrupts his peaceful life with a baby and the shadow of a deadly stalker, forever changing how Chehnuh sees his own past, humanity, and the heroic role he has yet to play in today's world.

Byrne

Imagination is survival. That's what he tells them. Full of weird quirks and crazy story ideas, novelist Maddox Byrne can't figure out how to connect with normal people. Ever since the lockdown began and the residents of Tower 881 were trapped together, all he's wanted was to keep morale high and finally get the woman of his dreams to notice him. But every person has a breaking point. Every person longs for what they can't have. How long can humanity live in distrust and paranoia? How long before every person loses their mind? Imagination. Imagination is survival. But can it really save us?

www.ingramcontent.com/pod-product-compliance
Lightning Source LLC
Chambersburg PA
CBHW021157010826
48971CB00014B/2683